MARVEL
IRON MAN

AN ORIGIN STORY

Bath • New York • Cologne • Melbourne • Delhi
Hong Kong • Shenzhen • Singapore

This is Tony Stark. Tony is usually a normal guy – only with a lot more money.

But when Tony puts on his special armour, he becomes more powerful than most other people. He even has a different name. When Tony puts on his armour, he becomes ...

Tony wasn't born a super hero. He hasn't always fought to protect people. But with villains on the loose, like Titanium Man and Iron Monger – who use Tony's technology for their own evil purposes – Tony feels it is his responsibility to stop them.

Tony didn't always get the job done this easily. Or this well. Tony's armour wasn't always so sleek. In fact, when he first became Iron Man, Tony's armour didn't even shine!

But if you really want to know how Iron Man was born, you need to start with the man behind the mask. You need to start with Tony.

Tony had so much money that he could go anywhere he wanted.

He loved to have fun. And he loved the finer things in life.

But Tony also worked hard. He was a brilliant inventor and he knew all sorts of things about science.

He loved to work with magnetic fields. Using them, he created a powerful energy force that he called 'repulsor technology'.

The military was interested in Tony's work. In fact, it was in a secret army lab that Tony's life was changed forever. An enemy army attacked and Tony was badly hurt!

Since Tony was famous, he was recognized straight away. The enemy knew all about his inventions. They threw him in a prison room filled with electronic and mechanical equipment. They wanted him to create a mighty weapon for them.

To make things worse, they told Tony that his heart had been hurt in the blast. He didn't have much longer to live.

Tony soon found he was not alone in the cell. The enemy had captured another famous scientist – Professor Yinsen. The enemy wanted the two men to work together on the great weapon.

But Professor Yinsen had other ideas – he knew a way to keep Tony alive!

The two men worked tirelessly to create something that would save
Tony's life and, at the same time, help them to escape the prison.

Finally, the men completed the device that Tony would always need to wear on his chest, in order to keep his heart beating.
But that wasn't all they had created.

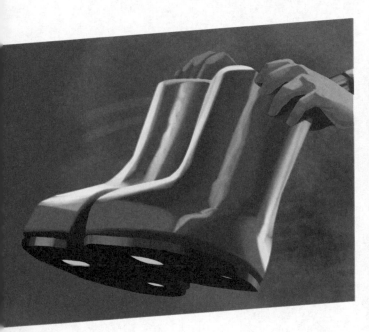

Using Tony's repulsor technology, they had built boots that could help a man fly!
Gloves that could crush steel!
And a helmet that could protect a man from the most terrible blast!

Tony put on the armour and proved that no walls could hold ...

… the Iron Man! It wasn't long before the enemy realized they were fighting a losing battle.

After escaping from prison, Tony flew home. But almost as soon as he got there, he realized that he could now help where others couldn't. He was strong, unstoppable and frightening.

But maybe he was a little too frightening.
Tony didn't want innocent people to be scared of him. He decided
the suit needed to change.

Tony thought that Iron Man needed something as smooth and as stylish as he was. He needed to create a lighter suit.

Although his chest plate couldn't change, everything around it could. Soon, Tony perfected the armour …

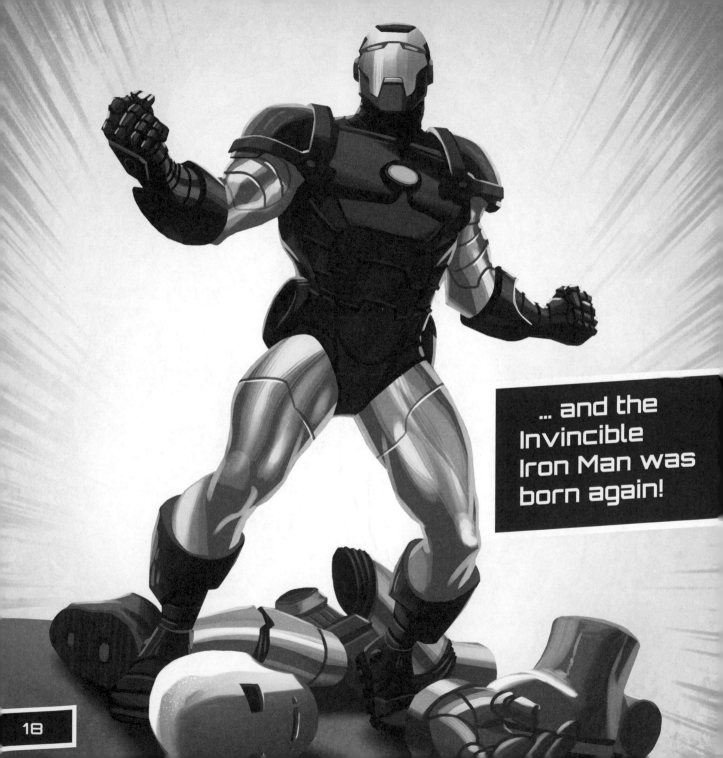

... and the Invincible Iron Man was born again!

As Iron Man, Tony never stops fighting. He protects people at home and around the world.

And when he's not fighting for justice as Iron Man …

… Tony runs his company, Stark Industries.

Stark Industries might need Tony to be a businessman, but with new villains attacking every day …

... the world needs Tony to be ...

... Iron Man!